Soggy Day at the Seaside

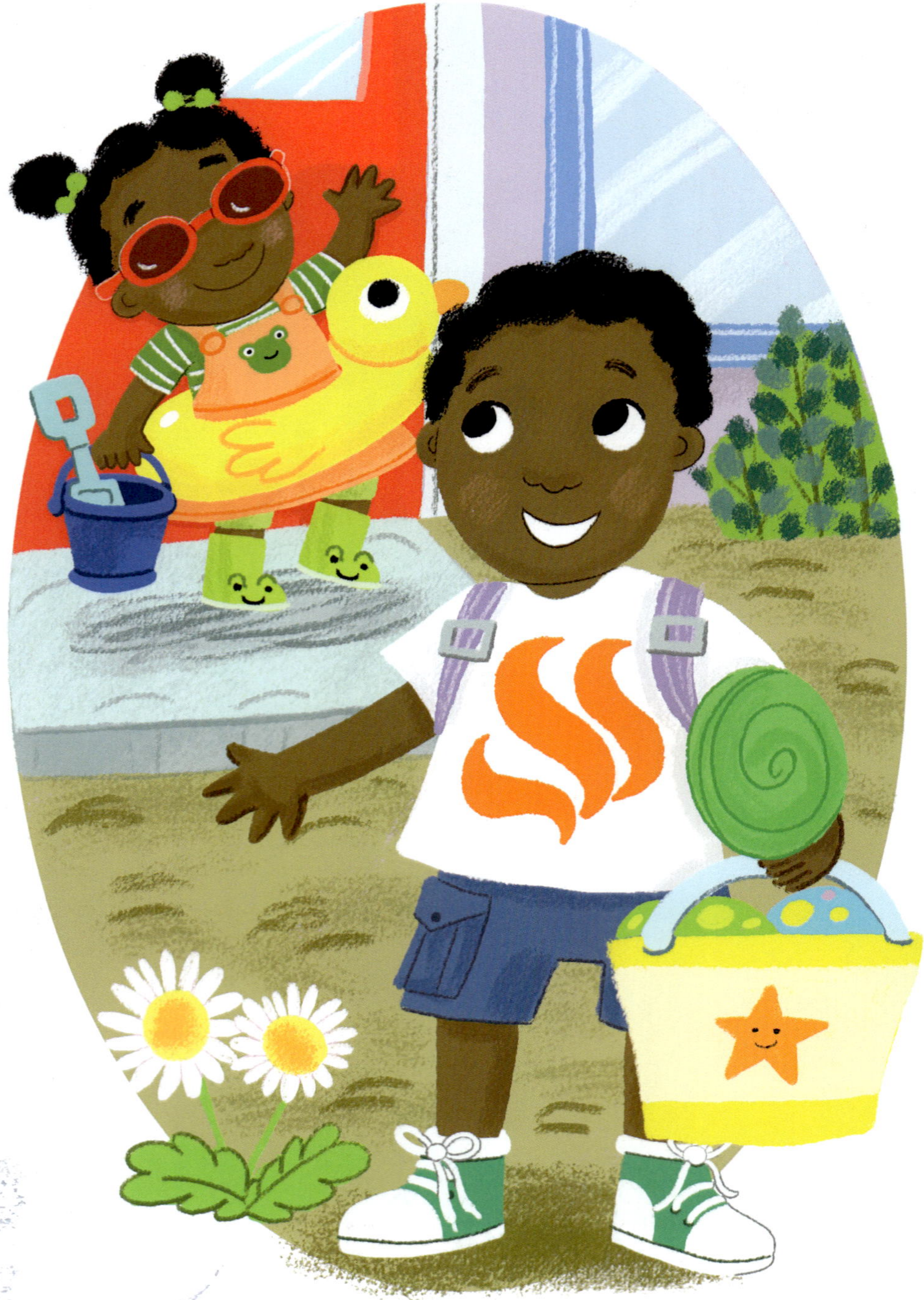

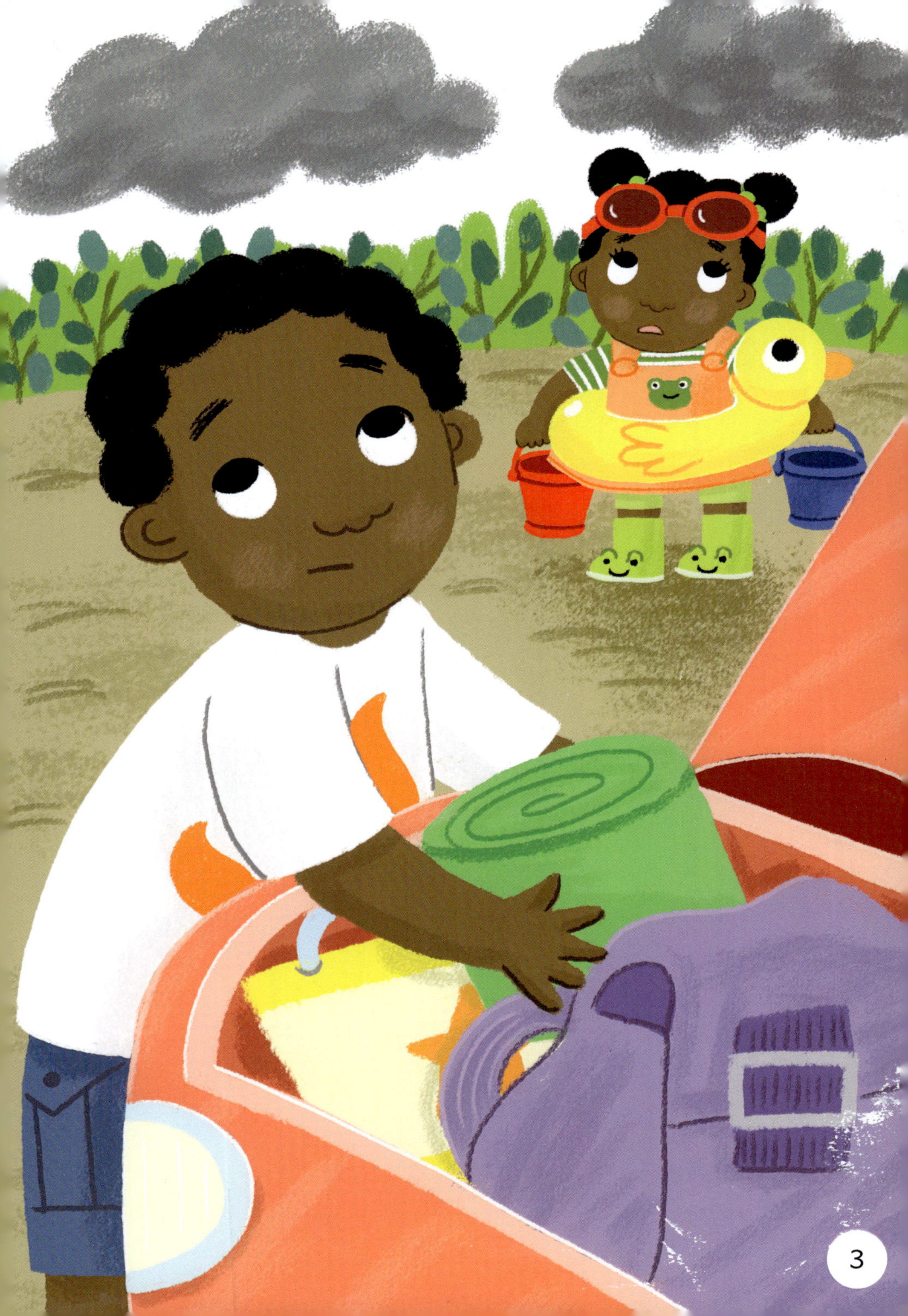

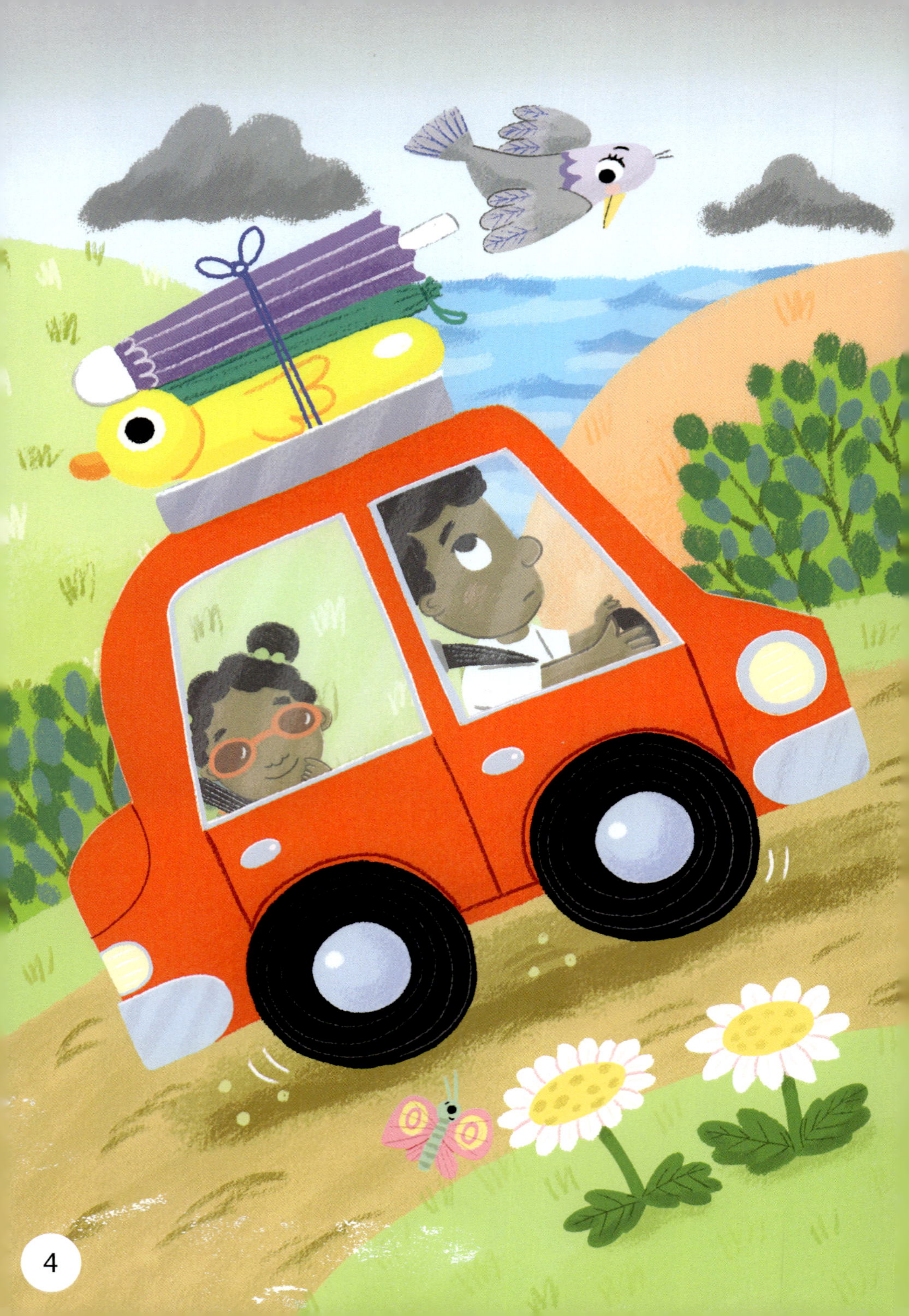

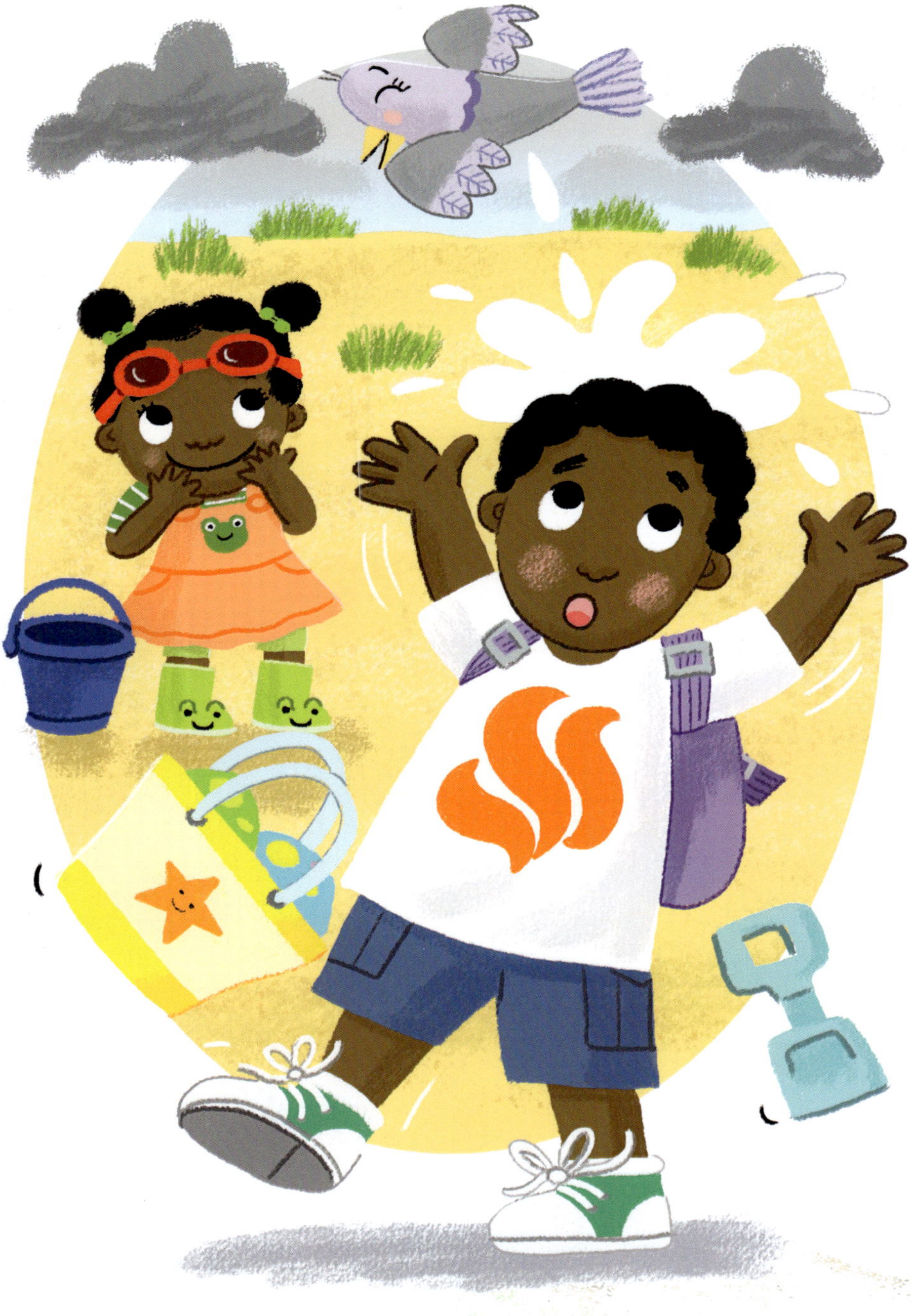

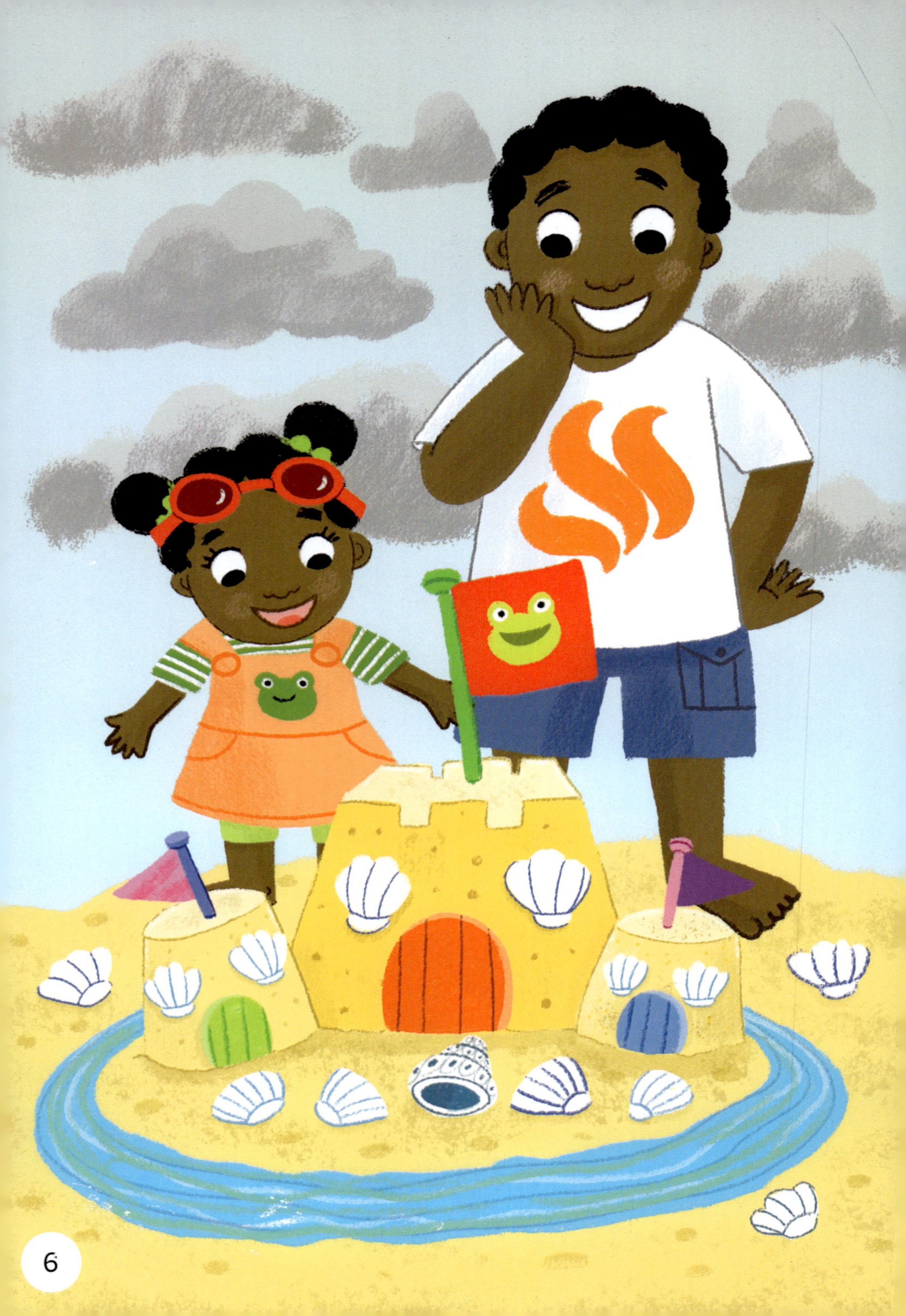

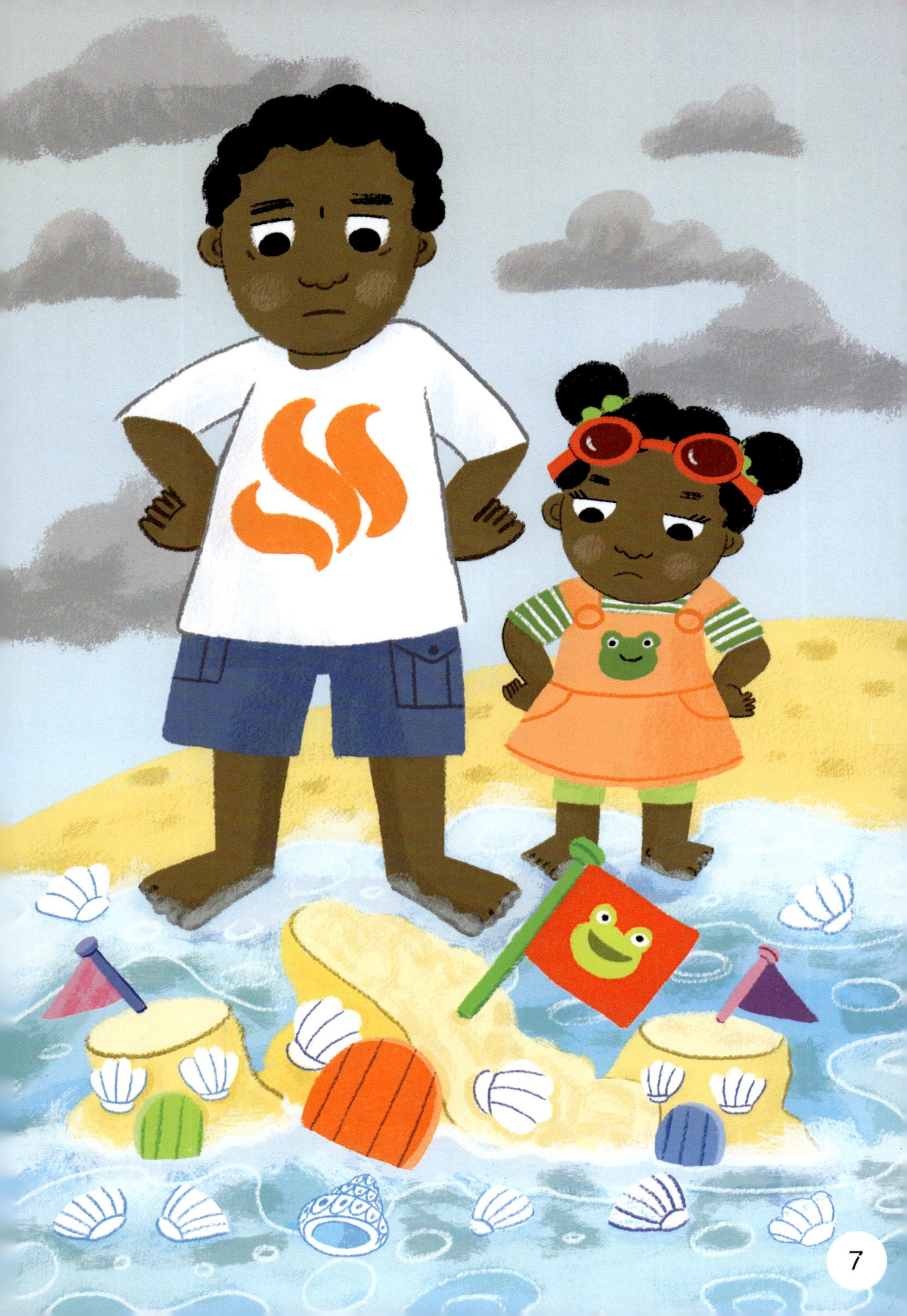

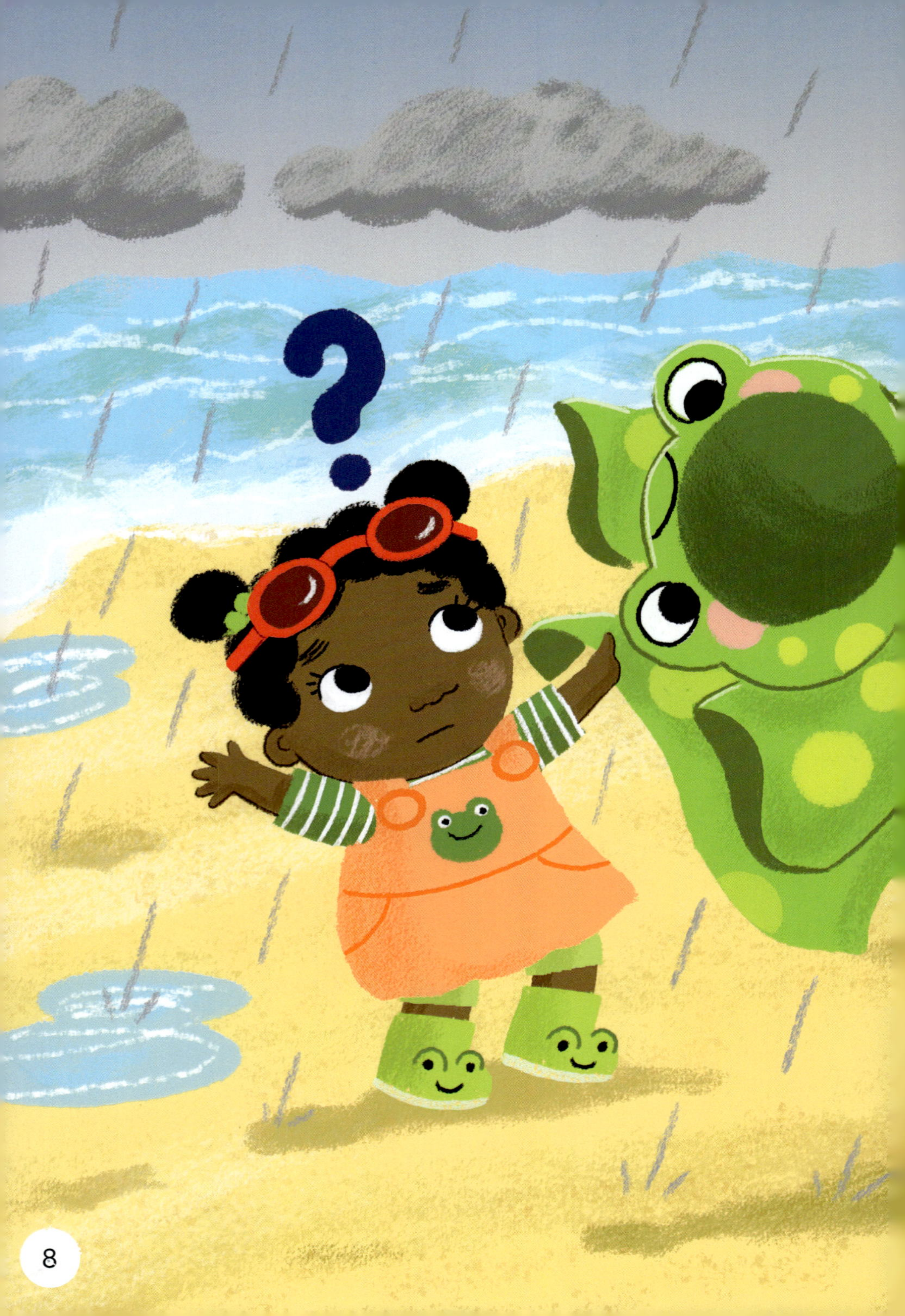

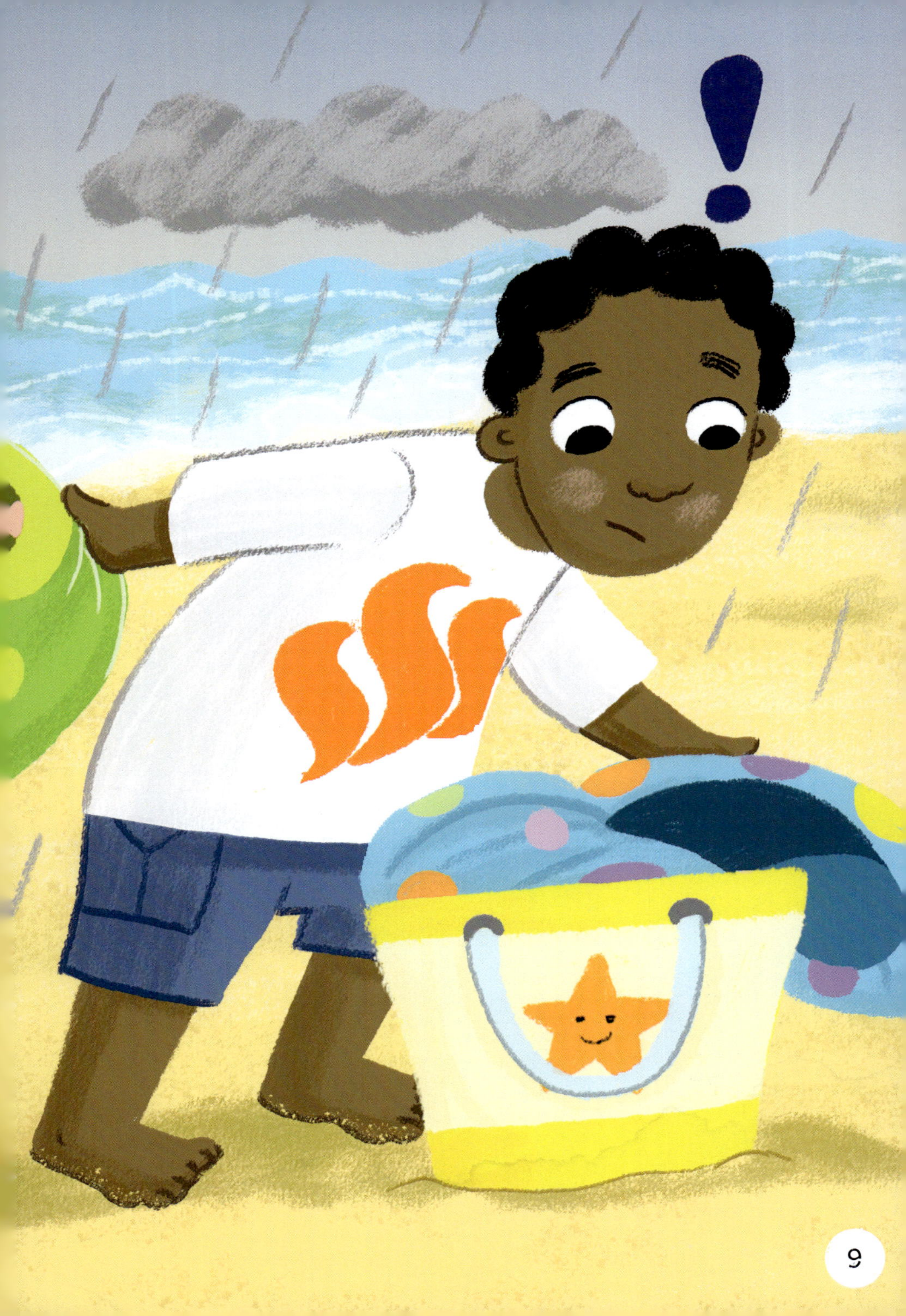

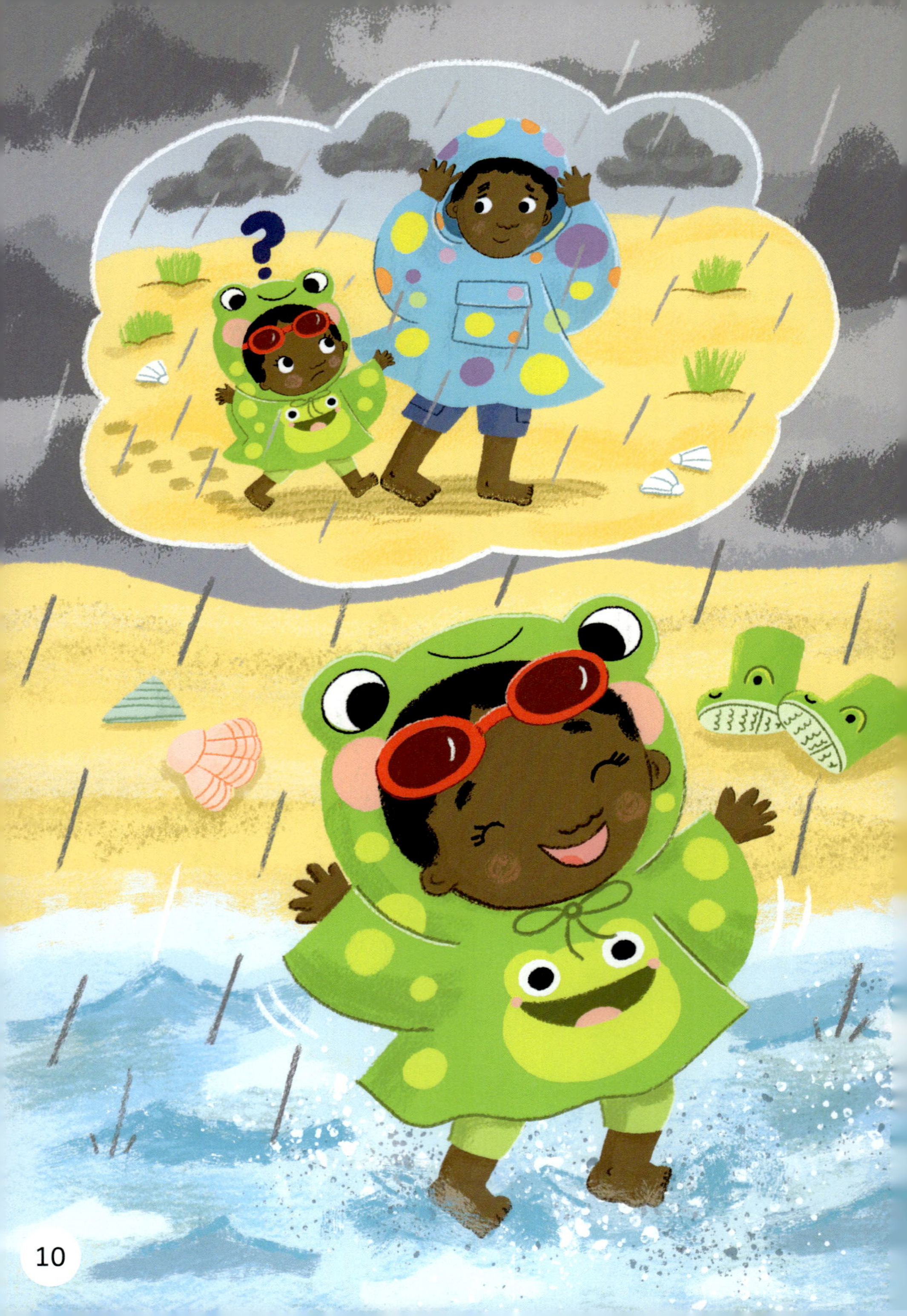

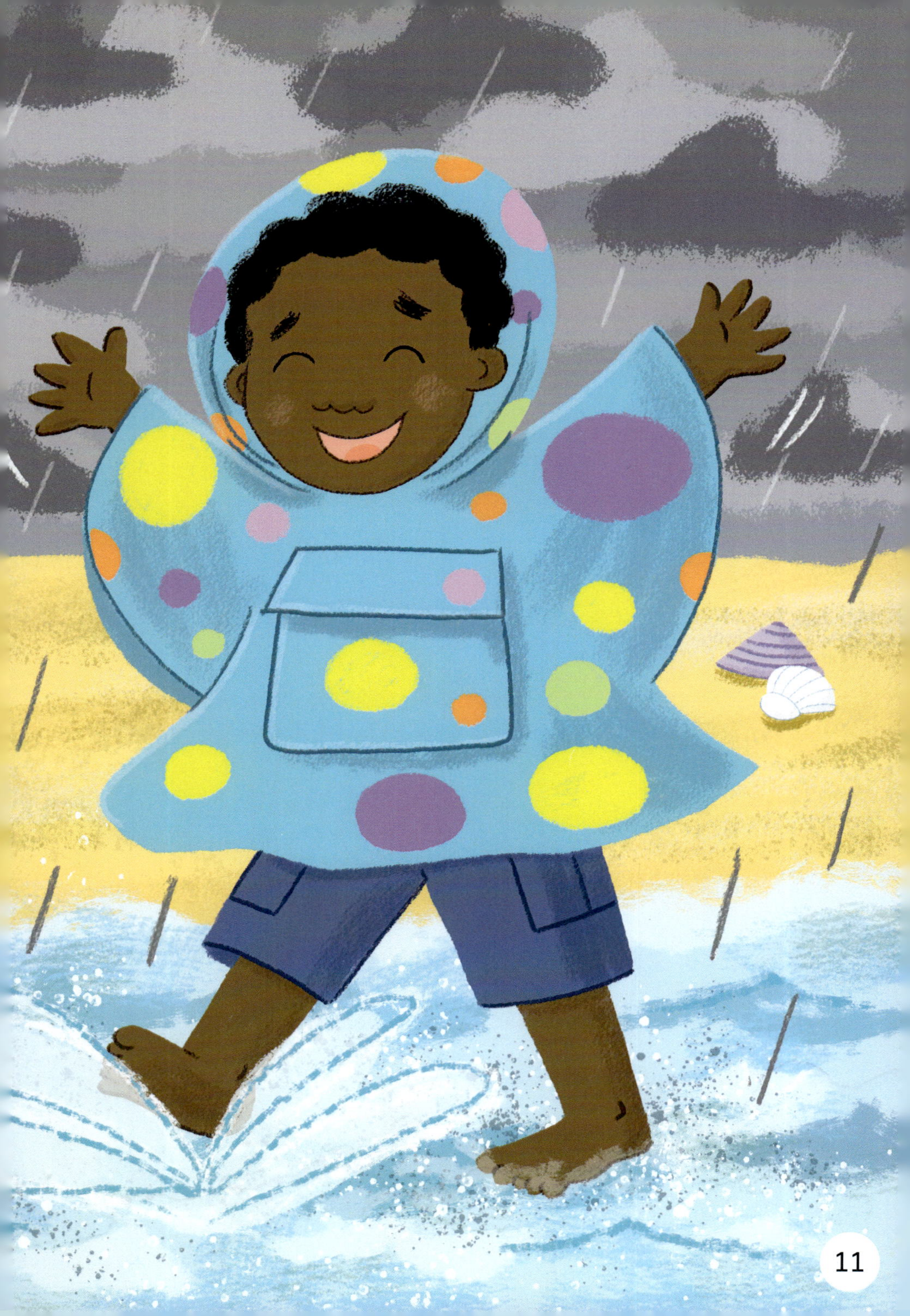

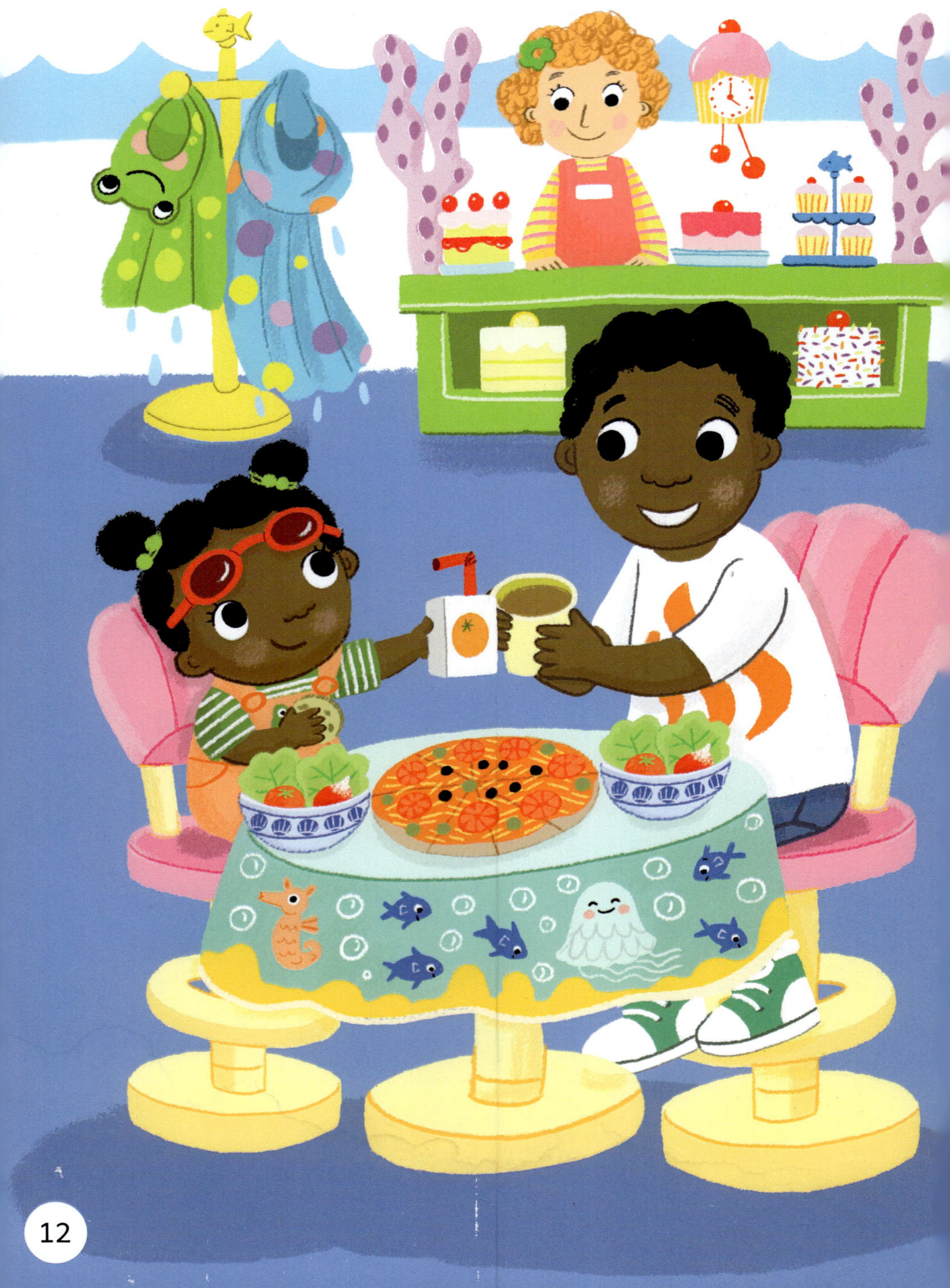